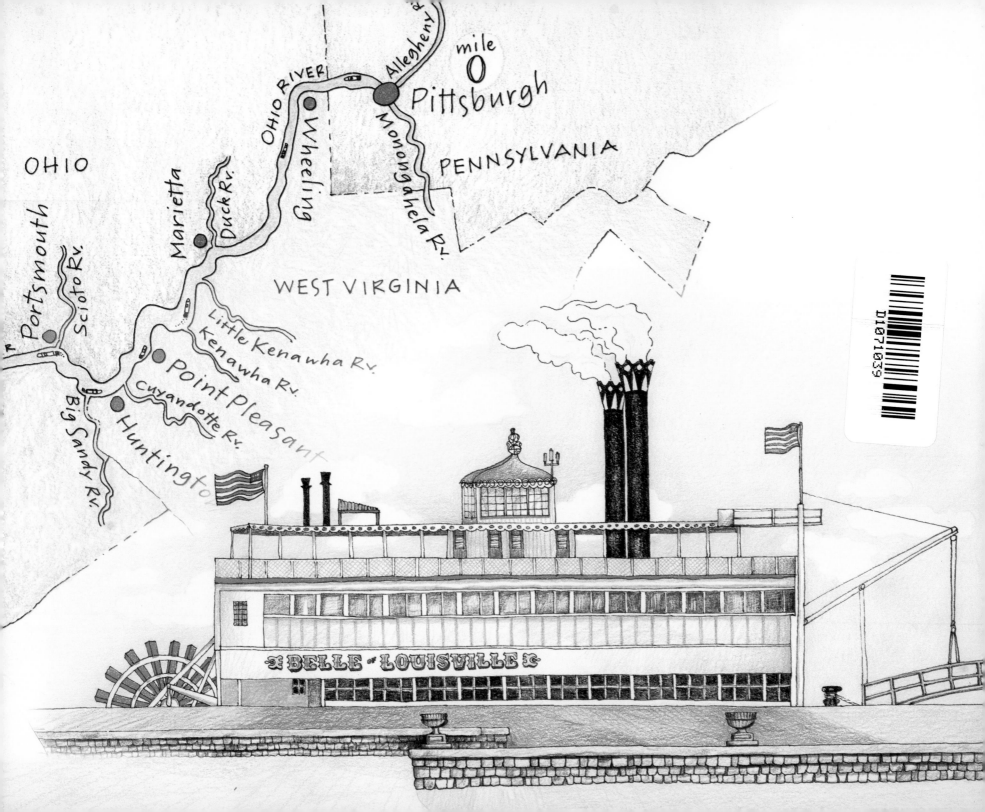

A Story Monsters Approved! book

ISBN: 978-0-692-64848-3

Library of Congress Control Number: 2016937299

Illustration and design: Susan Andra Lion
Sue Lion :: ink • Boulder, CO • 303-499-9891 • www.suelion.com

Distributed by Satiama, LLC. www.satiama.com

Summary: An adventurous cat takes four children on a tour of the *Belle of Louisville*, a historic steamboat operating in Louisville, Kentucky. Included is educational information about the Ohio River, how the mechanics of the boat work, and a thorough glossary of terms.

1. Children. 2. History. 3. Transportation. 4. Steamboat *Belle of Louisville*

Printed in China

Nosey's Wild Ride
on the *Belle of Louisville*

Martha Driscoll

Designed and Illustrated by Susan Andra Lion

About the Belle of Louisville

The *Belle* is not just a pretty girl; she's a beautiful old steamboat. She celebrated her 100th birthday in 2014. The *Belle of Louisville* was built in 1914 at Pittsburgh, Pennsylvania. She is the oldest steamboat still plying the inland waterways of the United States. Most steamboats were wooden boats with wooden hulls and a lifespan of only three to five years. The *Belle*, with her steel hull, is the only steamboat still cruising that was actually built during the Great Age of Steamboats.

Originally called *Idlewild*, in 1948 she was renamed *Avalon*. In 1962, when the boat was destined for the scrap heap, Jefferson County, Kentucky bought her at auction, refurbished her, and renamed her *Belle of Louisville*. In 1989, she and her wharfboat, *Life-Saving Station #10*, were named National Historic Landmarks.

The *Belle* has worked on many rivers, including the Mississippi, Illinois, St. Croix, Missouri, Cumberland, Kanawha, and Ohio. She has also done several important jobs. At Memphis, Tennessee, where there was no bridge crossing the Mississippi River, the *Belle* ferried passengers, wagons, and livestock from one riverbank to the other. Before there were fast trains, big trucks, and interstate highways to move heavy loads of freight, the *Belle* was a packet boat. She hauled cargo such as lumber, bales of cotton, boxes of household goods, and crates of farm produce from river town to river town.

Now the *Belle* is an excursion steamboat carrying passengers on cruises on the Ohio River. She travels upriver between Louisville, Kentucky, and Jeffersonville, Indiana. She travels downriver through the Portland Canal and McAlpine Locks and past McAlpine Dam and ancient fossil beds to western Louisville.

over
100
years old!

Dedication

This book is dedicated to my family, whose generosity, support, and understanding helped me finish this story.

Acknowledgements

With deepest appreciation and heartfelt thanks to the following individuals for their in-depth critiques and wise advice—
Kadie Engstrom, Sue Lion, Vicki Reed, Holly Holland, John Herzfeld, Lucinda Garthwaite, Sharon England,
Barbara and Clay Morris, and Anne Sabetta

About the Author

Martha Driscoll has had a longtime love affair with the *Belle*. As a child, she and her family enjoyed many picnic cruises
downriver on the *Idlewild*. As a teenager, her Jeffersonville, Indiana, high school senior prom was on the steamboat.
Martha and her husband attended many moonlight cruises on the boat when it was known as the *Avalon*.
In 1962, when Judge Marlow Cook called for assistance in refurbishing the *Belle*, Martha volunteered to help paint her.
For 27 years, Martha taught reading education at Spalding University. She has lived in Louisville, Kentucky, for 50 years.
Martha is 88 years old and vision impaired. She still enjoys cruises on the Ohio River and the ambiance of the *Belle*.
Nothing thrills her more than hearing the calliope playing tunes on a summer evening.

Kids, take your own tour of the Belle.
Find all the drawings in the Seek & Find
game pieces on each page. Have fun!

"Hey, come on. Hurry up! We're going for a ride on the *Belle of Louisville*," Al said to his younger sister Rosie.

"I can't wait. I've always wanted to take a ride on a big, old steamboat," Rosie replied. She climbed into the back seat of the car behind Al, who was old enough to drive. They fastened their seatbelts and were off. Al went five houses down to pick up their friend Martina. Then he drove around the corner to pick up their friend Jamal. Everyone was excited to be starting the day's adventure.

Al drove downtown to the banks of the Ohio River where the *Belle* was docked. The group of friends got out of the car at the Fourth Street wharf and walked across the cobblestones. They heard the calliope playing the tune "Alexander's Ragtime Band," then they saw the big boat.

Two tall smokestacks and a pilothouse topped her roof. A big red paddlewheel was partially submerged at her stern. Flags fluttered on her upper deck. She gleamed white with red and blue trim, and her name, *Belle of Louisville*, shone in large gold letters above her forward doors and along both sides.

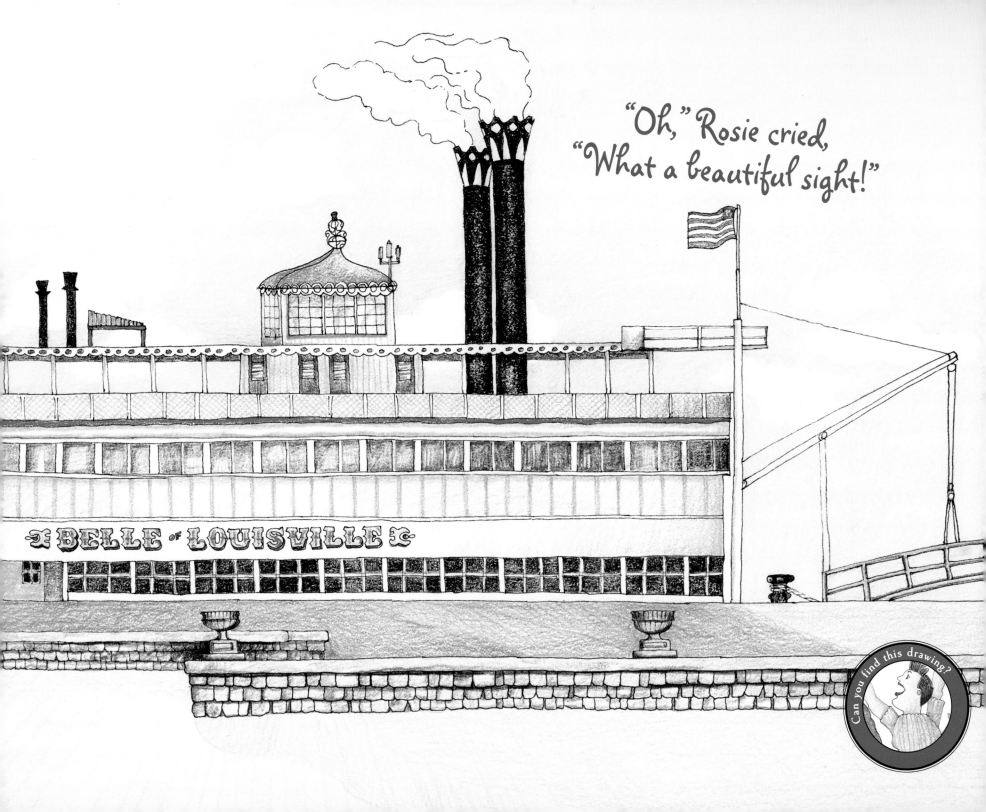

They hurried along and bought tickets at the wharfboat. Then they waited in a long line of people to board the steamboat.

"How far are we going?" Jamal asked.

"Not very far," Al said. "The Ohio River is so long that the *Belle* could never travel the length of it in one day."

"How long is the river?" Rosie asked.

"The Ohio runs for 981 miles from Pittsburgh, Pennsylvania, to Cairo, Illinois, where it empties into the Mississippi," Al replied. "It flows past six states – Pennsylvania, West Virginia, Kentucky, Ohio, Indiana, and Illinois."

INDIANA

ILLINOIS

White Rv.

Wabash Rv.

Pigeon Rv.

Evansville

OHIO RIVER

OHIO RIVER

New Albany

Clarksville

Jeffersonville

Madison

Rising Sun

Cincinnati

Licking Rv.

New

Harrods Cr.

Beargrass Cr.

Louisville
mile
606

Salt Rv.

Rolling Fork Rv.

Floyd's Fork

Henderson

Panther Rv.

Owensboro

Brandenburg

mile
981
Cairo

Mississippi Rv.

Paducah

Tennessee Rv.

Ky Lake

Cumberland Rv.

Lake Barkley

KENTUCKY

MISSOURI

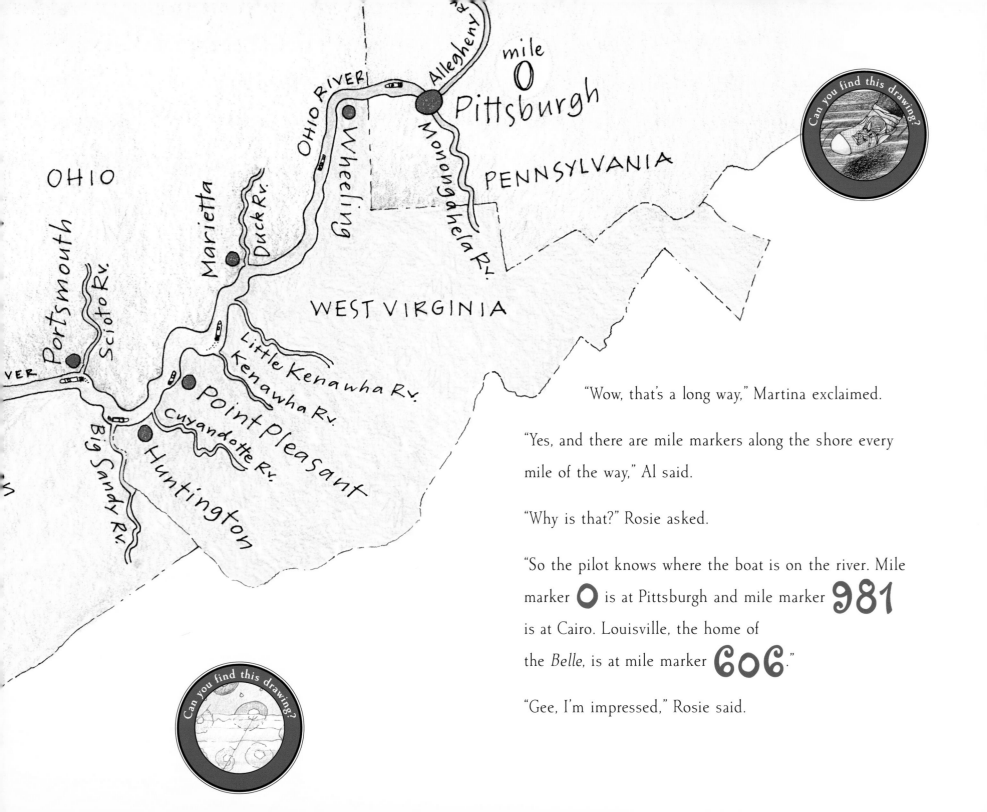

OHIO

OHIO RIVER

PENNSYLVANIA

mile
0
Pittsburgh

Allegheny R.

Monongahela R.

Wheeling

Marietta

Duck R.

WEST VIRGINIA

Portsmouth

Scioto R.

Little Kenawha R.

Kenawha R.

Point Pleasant

Cuyandotte R.

Huntington

Big Sandy R.

VER

Can you find this drawing?

Can you find this drawing?

"Wow, that's a long way," Martina exclaimed.

"Yes, and there are mile markers along the shore every mile of the way," Al said.

"Why is that?" Rosie asked.

"So the pilot knows where the boat is on the river. Mile marker **0** is at Pittsburgh and mile marker **981** is at Cairo. Louisville, the home of the *Belle*, is at mile marker **606**."

"Gee, I'm impressed," Rosie said.

Can you find this drawing?

While they watched the people ahead of them board the boat, Jamal said, "Hey, look. There's a cat on the gangway."

"Yeah, he's walking along with the people," Martina said.

"He's sneaking onto the boat!" Jamal cried.

"I think he's just nosing around and wants to know what's going on," Al said.

Rosie laughed and said, "O.K., then let's call him Nosey."

Finally it was their turn to walk up the gangway. As they handed their tickets to the deckhand who stood by the forward doors, Martina pointed at a pair of large golden antlers hanging on the wall. "What's that?"

"That's the trophy for the winner of the Great Steamboat Race, when the *Belle* used to race another steamboat called the *Delta Queen*," said Al.

Hey, there's a CAT!

As the line inched forward,
Jamal watched Nosey **run**
up the main staircase

STR. BELLE OF LOUISVILLE

Can you find this drawing?

and disappear

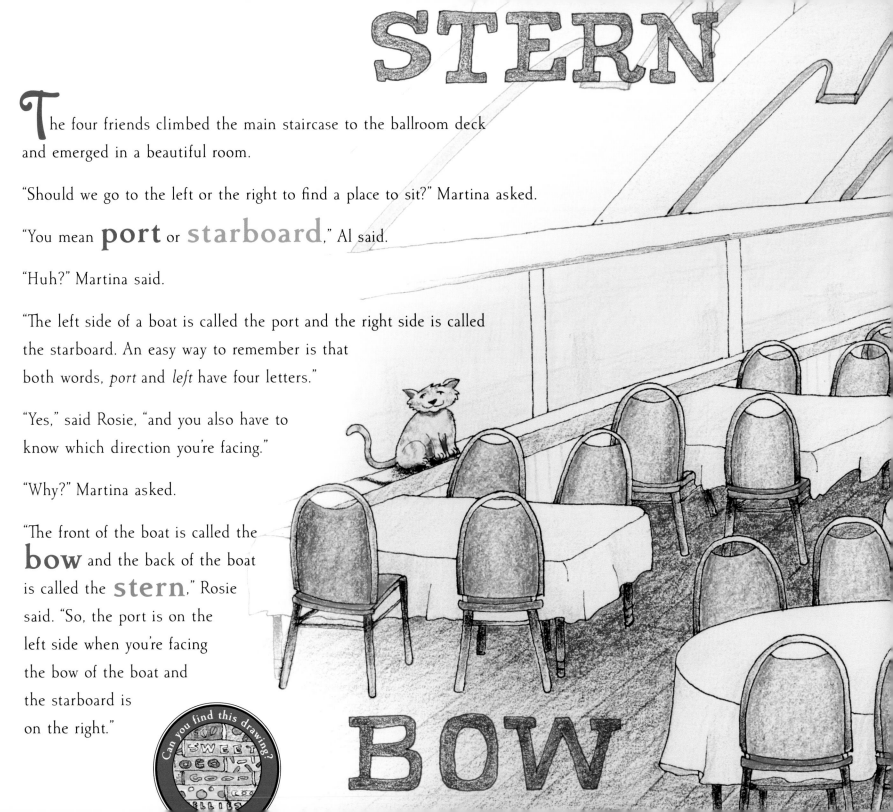

The four friends climbed the main staircase to the ballroom deck and emerged in a beautiful room.

"Should we go to the left or the right to find a place to sit?" Martina asked.

"You mean **port** or starboard," Al said.

"Huh?" Martina said.

"The left side of a boat is called the port and the right side is called the starboard. An easy way to remember is that both words, *port* and *left* have four letters."

"Yes," said Rosie, "and you also have to know which direction you're facing."

"Why?" Martina asked.

"The front of the boat is called the **bow** and the back of the boat is called the **stern**," Rosie said. "So, the port is on the left side when you're facing the bow of the boat and the starboard is on the right."

BOW

Long tables lined each
side of the ballroom dance floor.
The group of friends found a table and
chairs near a starboard window where they sat.

Are you wondering why port means left but it's on the
right side of this page? Remember that port and
starboard have to do with the location
of the bow and stern of the boat.

clang
clang
clang

Soon they heard the captain ring the roof bell three times to signal the crew to be ready to shove off. Then he called, "Let go the stern line," and a deckhand raced across the gangway and down the wharf to untie the line.

Can you find this drawing?

STR. BELLE
Can you find this drawing?

Then the deckhand ran back on board the boat. The stern line had kept the back of the boat from swinging out into the river. Two lines off the bow, the head line and the check line, kept the *Belle* tied to the wharfboat.

After the bow lines were untied by the watchman on the wharfboat, the *Belle* began to back out into the river, and the captain called to the pilot, *"ALL GONE."* The deckhands pulled the lines in and coiled them neatly on the boat's deck. The *Belle* was floating free and ready to head upriver under her own steam.

"What's that sound?" Martina asked.

"That's the boat's whistle," Al said. "The pilot is blowing a signal to let everyone know we a re leaving the wharf."

Steam hissed, the pitman arms moved, the paddlewheel turned

and the steamboat headed up river. The deckhands swung the gangway to the center of the bow to secure it. At last, the cruise was underway.

As the *Belle* got going, Nosey wove between the tables. Suddenly, whoosh, he was skidding across the waxed dance floor on his belly.

"Look at that silly cat slide," Jamal said.

When Nosey came to a stop, he gingerly got up on all four paws. Martina, Rosie, and Jamal hurried from the table to pick up Nosey, but as they ran toward him, he careened to the end of the dance floor. Suddenly, it seemed like all four were dancing together:

Can you find this drawing?

Two steps to the left,
two steps to the right,
two steps to the left,
two steps to the right,
one, two, three, four,
one two, three, four,
left, right, left right.

People clapped and
laughed at their antics and
then clapped some more.

Can you find this drawing?

Can you find this drawing?

ooops

grab that furball!

what a rascal cat!

Nosey scampered towards the concession stand, where boxes of gummi fish and sour balls were stacked in a pyramid on the top of the counter. *Crash-bam!* Nosey knocked off the boxes. The contents clattered to the floor, and candy scattered in all directions. People whipped around to see what was happening.

Nosey turned and disappeared down the stairs to the main deck.

look at that goofy cat!

workout cat - cool

hey, save some for me!

mine mine

The friends followed and saw Nosey dash along the starboard walkway and into the spotless engine room. The knobs and handles on all the machinery were brightly polished. The chief engineer picked up a broom to shoo away the cat. Nosey spun around and jumped on a pitman arm.

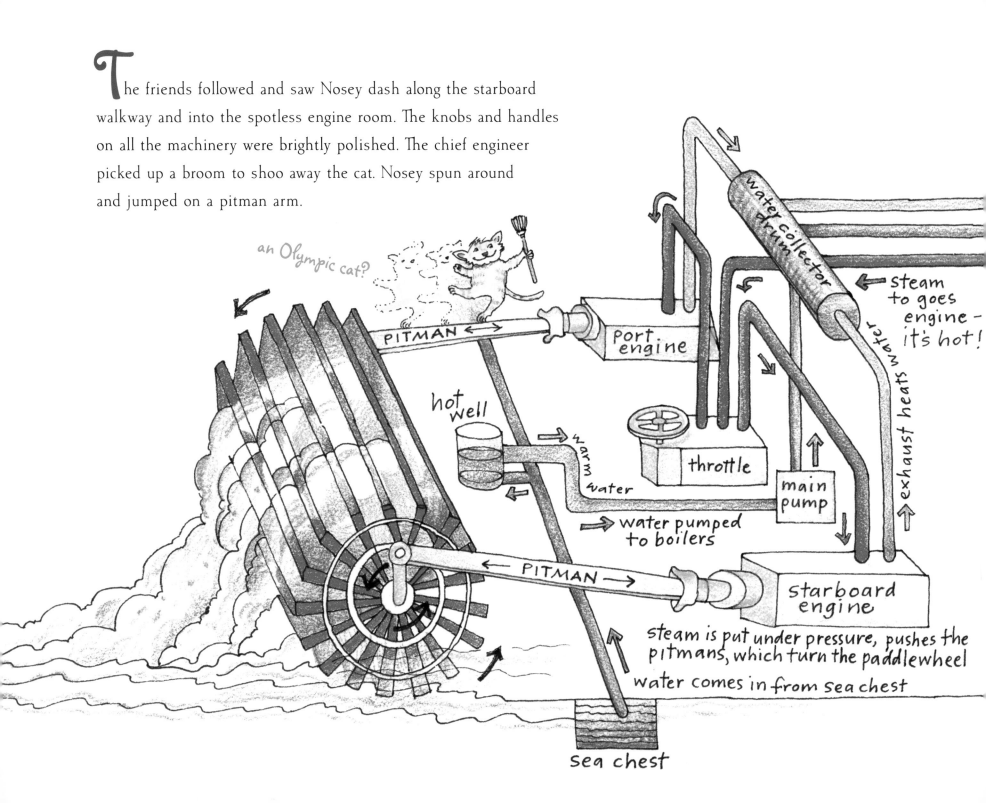

an Olympic cat?

PITMAN

port engine

water collector drum

steam to goes engine - it's hot!

hot well

warm water

exhaust heats water

throttle

main pump

water pumped to boilers

PITMAN

starboard engine

steam is put under pressure, pushes the pitmans, which turn the paddlewheel

water comes in from sea chest

sea chest

Can you find this drawing?

Pitman arms are long horizontal beams that attach an engine to each side of the paddlewheel. As the two arms glide back and forth, just like pedals on a bicycle, they turn the giant 24-foot paddlewheel, and the boat moves forward or backward through the water.

Nosey walked along the pitman arm as if it were a balance beam.

"Get off there, you crazy cat!"
the striker cried.

Nosey jumped off the pitman arm and darted past the galley and into the boiler room. It was steaming hot. The river water collected through the sea chest in the boat's hull was heated in the boilers and turned into steam. The steam powered the engines that made the paddlewheel turn and produced electricity for the boat. Without steam, the boat couldn't run, lights couldn't light, whistles couldn't blow, and the calliope couldn't play.

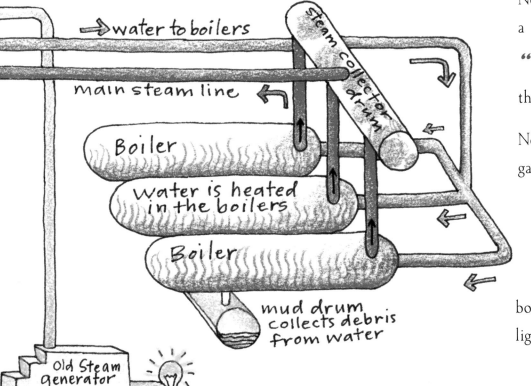

water to boilers

Steam collector drum

main steam line

Boiler

Water is heated in the boilers

Boiler

mud drum collects debris from water

Old Steam generator

The old steam generator made electricity for the Belle. But now, the Belle uses a different larger generator.

The fireman wanted Nosey out of the way. He needed to keep track of the steam levels so the boilers wouldn't **blow up.**

"Scat, you darn cat!"

Nosey bolted up the portside steps to the ballroom and flew back to the concession stand and souvenir shop. The friends followed him.

"Wow! That's one *speedy* cat," Martina said.

Jamal stopped at the concession stand to buy popcorn.
He gave some to Al. Al tossed a piece of popcorn to the cat.

Nosey jumped up and caught it.

Al kept tossing more popcorn and Nosey
kept **leaping** to snatch it out of the air.

Passengers stared in amazement.

good catch

bravo

yummy!

When the popcorn was gone,
Nosey flicked his tail, took
a side step, and ran up the
stairway to the texas deck where
the boat's only cabin was located.

The four friends chased after Nosey...again.

Nosey spied the captain coming out of his cabin, and slipped into the room before the captain closed the door.

The captain heard,

"Meow, meow, meow."

He said, "Where's the cat?"

"He's in your cabin," Al answered.

"How did he get in there?" asked the captain.

"He snuck into the room while you weren't looking," Rosie said.

"Oh, no," the captain said.

"Get that sneaky cat out of there!"

When the captain opened the door, Al made a grab for Nosey,
but the cat ducked and ran toward the chairs near the bow
and hid underneath one of them.

"I can see him," cried Jamal, as he stretched to reach for Nosey.
But the cat kept moving backward out of Jamal's reach,
and bumped into a lady's feet.

She screamed, kicked up her heels, and knocked over her chair.
It was *bedlam* as other people jumped
up to see what was happening.

Nosey went *zip* and scooted
away. The friends followed right
behind him.

They thought they were on a cruise up the lazy river, but it was turning out to be a *wild* afternoon chase instead.

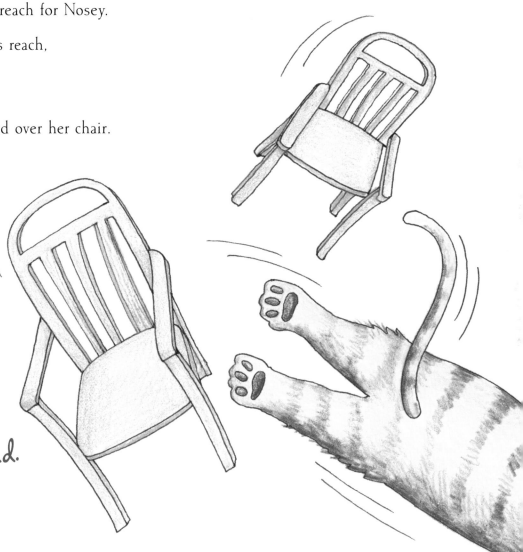

Nosey ran towards the stern. He jumped on a table where a family was enjoying glasses of cool lemonade. He knocked over their drinks and got everybody wet. Boy, were they mad.

"Grab that little scamp," cried the father, but Nosey jumped off the table and ran down three steps to the hurricane deck.

Nosey stopped by the fence railing overlooking the paddlewheel. He seemed momentarily hypnotized by the motion of the paddlewheel as it went **swish, swish, swishing** through the water.

Al, Rosie, Martina, and Jamal hurried to catch up with Nosey. They felt the cool spray of water from the paddlewheel on their arms and faces.

"It makes me dizzy to watch the paddlewheel," Martina said.

"Yeah, but I like to watch the wake the paddlewheel leaves behind the steamboat," Jamal said.

"I like to feel the wind blowing in my hair," Rosie said with a sigh.

Nosey got up, stretched, and strolled off toward the texas deck. Near the Captain's Quarters, he noticed an open door. Behind the door were ten steep steps leading up to the hatch on the steamboat's roof.

"Look, Nosey is heading up those steps," Jamal shouted.
They scrambled to follow the cat.

The door to the pilothouse was open. The pilothouse was a small glass-enclosed room on top of the boat from which the pilot could look out to see the river in all directions. The pilothouse contained all of the controls. There the pilot stood behind a seven-foot pilot wheel to steer the boat.

When Nosey got inside the pilothouse, he tried to jump on the pilot wheel, but fell off. He picked himself up and tried again.

The pilot swatted at Nosey and shouted, "Skedaddle, cat!"

Nosey bounded out of the pilothouse and darted toward the flagpole on the stern of the roof. He ran so fast that he ran **smack** right into the pole.

Can you find this drawing?

BELLE of LOUISVILLE

Nosey picked himself up and sprinted toward the calliope. He took a running leap and landed on top of the steam whistles while the calliopist was playing "Maple Leaf Rag." The 32 steam whistles were really loud and blistering hot. Nosey shrieked in surprise, "Yowie, yowie, yowie!" To keep from burning his paws he launched himself into the air, whipped around, and whizzed toward the roof's bow.

yowie!
yowie!
yow

Nosey stopped and hid behind the boat's big roof bell. While he crouched there trying to catch his breath, the pilot rang the bell. Scared by the sound, Nosey hurled himself toward the starboard side of the roof and fell off. People who saw him falling down, down, down past the decks cried, "Oh no, oh no!" The captain stepped out on a wing bridge to see what was happening. Suddenly, *ker-plop*, Nosey found himself in the river flailing and thrashing about.

"We've got to save that cat!" Martina shouted.

The friends turned and raced down the stairs to the main deck.

The pilot shouted to the chief engineer, "Stop the engines!" The giant paddlewheel stopped turning and the boat began drifting in the current of the river.

A deckhand grabbed a pole with a net on the end and tried to scoop up Nosey. But Nosey floated away from the steamboat and the deckhand accidentally dropped the pole in the river.

The four friends dashed onto the bow. Rosie kicked off her shoes and dove into the water to save the cat.

Another deckhand shouted, "Grab this ring!" and threw a life preserver on a line to Rosie. She caught the big orange donut and started to swim sidestroke toward Nosey. When she got close, she tried to grab the cat by the tail, but missed.

Rosie tried again, but Nosey wiggled away from her grasp, climbed over her shoulder, and onto the taunt line attached to the life preserver.

The cat tried walking back to the boat as if he were on a tightrope, but the line sagged and **ker-flop...**

Nosey was back in the water...AGAIN!

On the third try, Rosie caught
Nosey and stuffed him inside her shirt. Hand over
hand, the deckhand quickly hauled in the life preserver. When
Rosie and Nosey got back to the side of the steamboat, Al and the deckhand
reached down and plucked them out of the water and onto the bow.

Rosie pulled the bedraggled cat out of her shirt. Both she and
Nosey were a soggy mess. A deckhand handed Rosie a towel.
She dried Nosey off, gave him a kiss on the top of his head, and
handed him to Jamal. Then Rosie dried off her face and arms.

The first mate produced a mesh laundry bag and said to Jamal,
"Put that kooky cat in here to keep him safe."

The people on the boat cheered. "Hooray, hooray!
Rosie saved the day! She saved the cat!"

The pilot gave the signal to the chief engineer to start
the engines again. Soon the *Belle* was back at the wharf
and getting ready to dock.

The captain came over to Rosie and said, "I applaud you for
saving the cat." Then he placed a captain's cap on her head.
The people **whooped** and **hollered**, and **clapped**
and **cheered** some more for Rosie.

The pilot docked the steamboat at the wharf and a deckhand jumped off to tie up the stern of the boat. The gangway was lowered and people began streaming off the *Belle*. Jamal gently slung the laundry bag holding Nosey over his shoulder. Then Jamal, Rosie, Martina, and Al walked down the gangway to the wharf steps. Jamal knelt and let the cat out of the bag.

Nosey streaked up the levee and across River Road to who knows where. As the first mate leaned over the rail and watched Nosey go, he called out, "That was some mischievous cat!"

"Yep," Al said, "and he gave us a memorable cruise on the *Belle of Louisville!*"

Glossary

antlers: A set of large deer or elk horns painted gold and used as a trophy. The winner of the Great Steamboat Race that was held during the Kentucky Derby Festival, got to keep the trophy until the next year's race.

ballroom: A large dance floor

boiler room: Also called the firebox. This is where river water, taken in through the sea chest in the boat's hull, is heated to produce the steam that powers everything on the steamboat.

boilers: The three tanks on the *Belle* that hold the water that is heated to produce steam. The water in the boilers is heated by fire, just like a flame on a gas stove heating a tea kettle. The hot water builds up steam. The piping system puts the steam under pressure and then sends it to various locations on the boat.

calliope: A musical instrument on the roof of the *Belle*. It has 32 steam whistles that are played from a brass keyboard housed in a cupboard on the texas deck. The music of the calliope can be heard several miles away.

captain: The officer in command of the boat

Captain's Quarters: The only cabin on the *Belle*

chief engineer: The officer who is in charge of the engine room

cobblestones: Large rounded stones used for paving a street or levee

concession stand staff: The crew members who sell food, beverages, and souvenirs

crew: All the people who work on the boat:

- *officers:* Captain, pilot, first mate, chief engineer, and purser
- *other workers:* Deckhands, fireman, staff for concession and souvenir stands, and striker

deck: A floor on the boat:

- *main deck (first level):* Boiler room, engine room, galley, main staircase, and storage lockers
- *boiler deck* or *ballroom deck (second level):* Concession stand, dance floor, restrooms, and souvenir stand
- *hurricane deck* and *texas deck (third level):* Calliope keyboard, Captain's Quarters, stairs to the roof, and open-air and partially covered seating areas
- *roof (fourth level):* The top of the steamboat containing the calliope steam whistles, flagpole, searchlights, pilothouse, roof bell, boat's whistle, and smokestacks

deckhands: The crew members who handle the lines and maintain the boat

diesel oil: The fuel used to make the fire that heats river water in the *Belle's* boilers to create steam

engine: There are two engines on the *Belle*. They are the machines that turn the paddlewheel.

fireman: The crew member who lights and watches the fire in the firebox in order to maintain the steam pressure that powers the boat

first mate: The officer who is second in command and oversees maintenance of the boat

fuel tanks: The *Belle's* fuel tanks are in her hull. They hold 22,000 gallons of fuel oil. When she is running at normal speed, the *Belle* burns 150 gallons of fuel per hour.

galley: The kitchen on a boat

gangway: Also called the stage, passengers walk over this moveable walkway to get on or off the boat.

Great Steamboat Race: For 45 years, this annual race between two or three steamboats on the Ohio River at Louisville was part of the Kentucky Derby Festival.

hatch: An opening. Some hatches provide access to the hull; one hatch in the roof of the *Belle* provides access to the pilothouse.

hull: The bottom of a boat. The *Belle's* hull, which is made of steel, is where the sea chest is located and the fuel for her boilers is stored. Most of her hull cannot be seen because it is below the waterline.

hurricane deck: An open-air walkway that runs around the texas deck. It got its name because it is exposed to all kinds of weather and the wind can always be felt on this deck as passengers and crew travel up and down the river. It is also the longest continuous deck on the *Belle*.

inland waterway: All of the navigable rivers in the central part of the United States, including the Mississippi, Arkansas, Illinois, St. Croix, Missouri, Cumberland, Kanawha, and Ohio Rivers.

life preserver: A buoyant circular float with a line attached. The float is thrown to someone in the water and the line is used to haul the person to safety.

lines: All ropes, cables, or pipes used on a boat

mile markers: Numbered posts placed on the banks every mile along a river to help pilots know where they are

paddlewheel: The huge wooden wheel at the back of the *Belle*. It is made of the hardest wood that can be purchased in the United States, such as white oak. It weighs 17.5 tons, is 24 feet across, and 17 feet wide. It propels the steamboat forward or backward on the river.

pilot: The officer who steers the boat

pilothouse: A small glass-enclosed room on the roof of a steamboat from which the pilot can see in all directions while steering the boat. All controls for the steamboat are in the pilothouse.

pilot wheel: The seven-foot steering wheel on the *Belle*. The *Belle's* pilot wheel is as old as the boat.

pitman arms: Long beams on each side of the *Belle's* paddlewheel. Each attaches an engine to the paddlewheel shaft. The two pitman arms go back and forth to turn the paddlewheel, which moves the boat in the river.

purser: An officer who oversees the operations of concession and souvenir stands

rudders: A group of three large, thick panels that work together to turn the boat left or right. The pilot uses the pilot wheel to move the rudders, which are located at the bottom of the boat just in front of the paddlewheel.

sea chest: A tank in the steamboat's hull, below the waterline, through which river water is pumped into the boiler system where it is heated to produce steam

searchlights: The *Belle's* two strong, bright lights used to see through fog, scan the river, or see the shore and mile markers at night

she: A boat is always referred to as female, even if her name is a man's name like the steamboat *Robert E. Lee*.

smokestacks: Two tall pipes that reach high above the roof of the *Belle* from which smoke can escape from the boilers

steamboat: A large boat propelled by a steam-driven paddlewheel

Steamboat Era: This was a period ranging from the 1820s to the 1920s. It is also called the Great Age of Steamboats.

striker: A crew member who assists the engineer when the boat is under steam

texas deck: From the steamboat tradition of naming the highest deck on the boat after Texas, the largest state of the union in the 19th century

wake: The trail of water left by a steamboat as it cruises the river

wharf: A sloping cobblestone and concrete landing where the *Belle of Louisville* ties up

wharfboat: *Life-Saving Station #10* is the only floating life-saving station, and the last inland waterway life-saving station still in existence in the United States. Also named the *Mayor Andrew Broaddus*, she now serves as the wharfboat, ticket office, and offices for the staff and crew of the *Belle of Louisville*.

whistle: A means of communicating messages from an officer to the crew on a boat or between boats. The *Belle's* whistle is steam-powered.

wing bridges: Small stands on both the port and starboard sides that extend out from the roof so the captain can walk out to see over the bow of the steamboat

Can you find this drawing?

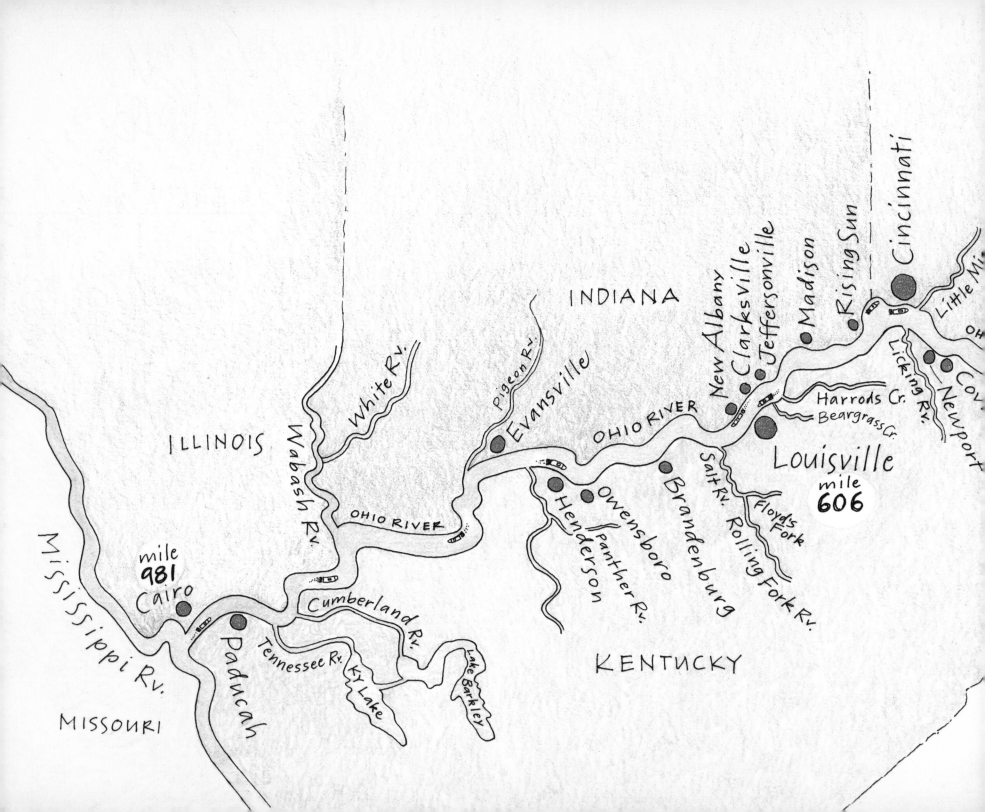